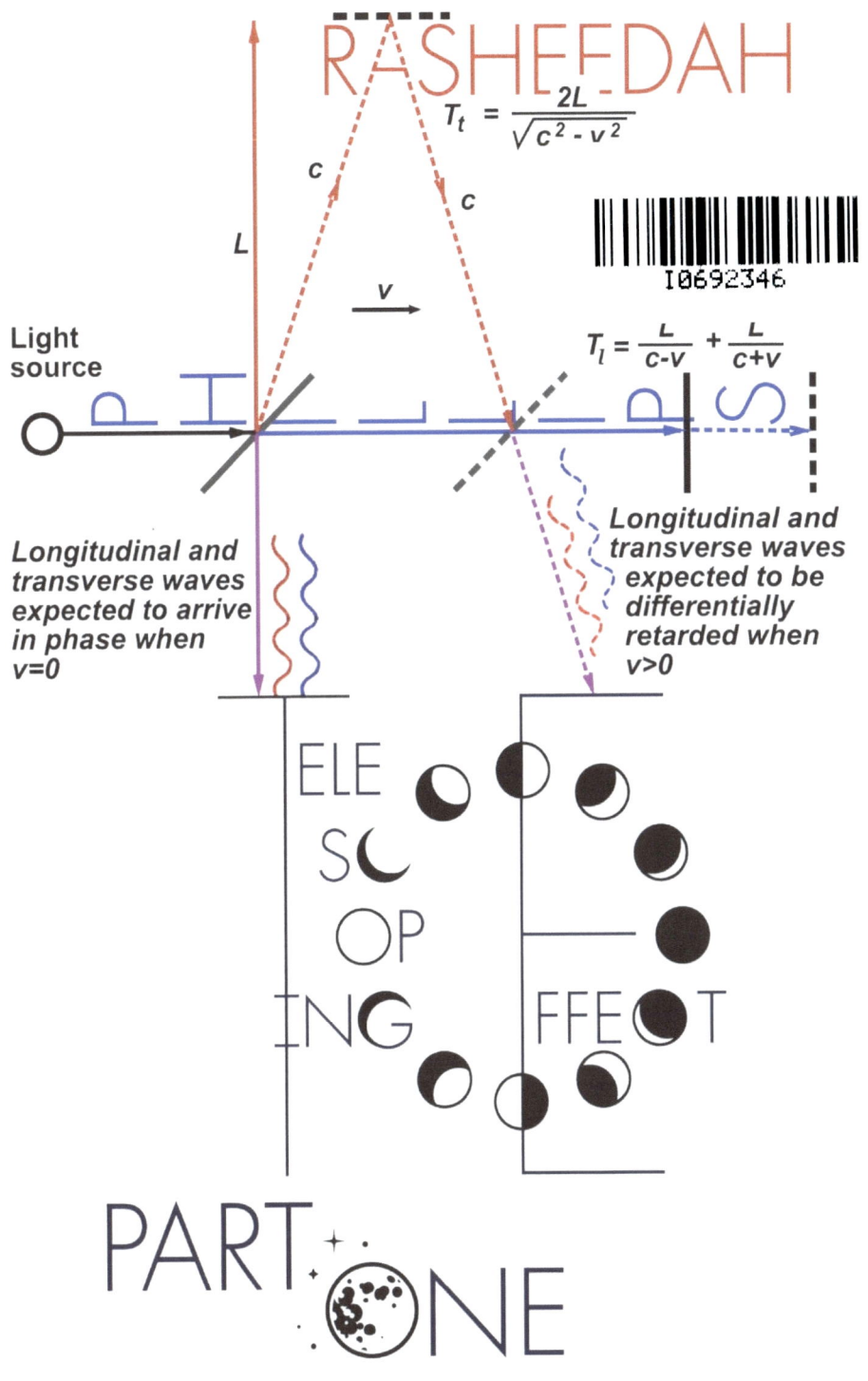

"The eclipse of the sun or moon is not simply a silent phenomenon of nature, but one that speaks to the community that observes it, often warning of an impending catastrophe."

— John S. Mbiti

I. CHARLESTON, SC: MAY 17, 1919

Shirley Ann almost didn't make it to Ma Belle's house this weekend because of the riots last Saturday, and she wasn't about to be sorry for it. Her mama had to work anyway. Even though the city was on something called a "martial law," the white lady was making mama come in to help with cleaning up the stores, so there was nothing Shirley Ann could do to avoid the trip. The rest of her brothers and sisters were old enough to stay home by themselves. But Shirley Ann, the baby of the house, had to be "babysat," and had to walk the two miles over there with her mama being her grumpy self.

Usually the only fun part about going to Ma Belle's house on a weekend was when she took her afternoon nap. Every Saturday and Sunday at noon, when her house clock chimed, Ma Belle would sit on the front porch of her house, smoke a cigarette, sip her fresh-squeezed lemonade, and pass out in her rocking chair, rain or shine.

It was then, and only then, that Shirley Ann could climb the seven creaky steps up to the dusty attic, where Ma Belle kept all her old heels and lab coats from her time working as a scientist, way back before Shirley Ann was born. She would try on the clothes and twirl in the big, heavy full-length mirror propped up against the wall, pretending she was in some white, shiny lab in a big city up north. Shirley Ann's mom sometimes told the story about how Ma Belle had been one of the first blacks, and one of the first women, to work in a science lab all the way up in Philadelphia.

But Ma Belle never talked much about that herself, or what she did now. A lot of it was just secrets and whispers, and her mama seemingly upset with her grandmother about one thing or another when she dropped Shirley Ann off to be minded.

This weekend was different, though. Instead of passing out on the porch at noon, Ma Belle and Shirley Ann had gone to the park not too far from her house to take some pictures up on the hill top.

And it seemed like it was going to be fun at first because she finally got to see Ma Belle's camera telescope thingy, which she kept locked up in a wooden box with the words NORTH STAR TRACKER carved on it in fancy gold lettering. Shirley Ann always saw the box tucked away in a dusty corner of the attic behind a curtain. She'd asked about it a dozen times, but Ma Belle always said it was too dangerous and delicate to touch, and then fussed at her for playing in the attic while she was napping.

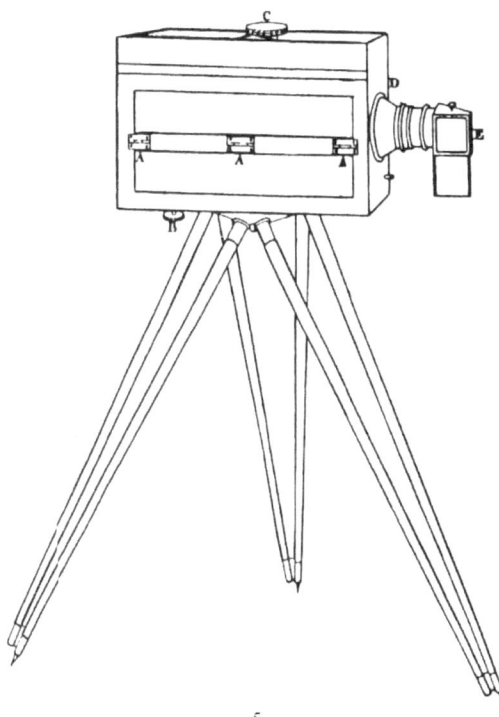

But now Shirley Ann was getting bored waiting for something to happen. They had been out in the park up on the hill top, and in the sun for what felt like hours. The box was on the ground over by her grandmother with the lid off, its contents assembled into what looked like a big box camera with a tube sticking out of it. Not that she had seen too many cameras in her nine years of life, but the ones she did see looked nothing like this. They were usually small enough to hang around your neck and carry around.

Shirley Ann sucked her teeth, asking, "What exactly is we waiting on, Ma Belle?" The sky was as still as the park around them. There was nothing she could see that was so interesting.

"A signal," Ma Belle said, not looking up from her camera, "I'm waiting for a signal, Shirley Ann. It'll be just a few minutes now. I need to expose the plate for a bit more, and I need you to write down some numbers for me when I get that signal." Shirley Ann watched her grandmother pull a small, clear, rectangular object out of the North Star Tracker. "I thought you wanted to help me out, girl."

"I do! We just been out here forever, that's all." Shirley Ann whined. She didn't know what "expose the plate" meant, but it sounded better than writing down some numbers like they was at school.

Earlier, she heard her mama and Ma Belle speaking in loud whispers about one of Ma Belle's assistants, Jamison, getting hurt real bad in the riot. Mama sounded upset talking about it, saying that, "No respectable negro shoulda been caught in that mess in the first place," and, "that's how them other three black boys ended up dead." Ma Belle told her that what was in the newspapers was a lie, and they always lied, and how if she read the colored folks news in Charleston, she would know the facts. "It weren't no colored boys who started it, girl."

REPORT·SIX KILLED IN SAILOR-NEGRO RIOT

Other Persons Are Wounded, Eight Severely, in a Race Clash at Charleston, S. C.

Charleston, S. C., May 10.—Beginning after a negro was accused of shooting down a bluejacket at Market and Beaufain streets, in a poolroom, serious race rioting in which bluejackets, assisted by some civilians, apparently, attacked many negroes, occurred here late last night and early this morning. Two bluejackets and four negroes are reported to have been killed, and more than eight men wounded severely, the Roper hospital being overwhelmed for a time.

Police were unable to stop the bluejackets from the naval training camp, and naval officers dispatched additional provost guards by motor car, while a detachment of marines was hurried into town to serve as a patrol. A little after midnight, because of the seriousness of the situation, policemen and marines instructed all persons in the streets to get home and stay there. Rear Admiral Benjamin C. Bryan, commandant of the navy yard, kept in as close touch as possible with the rioting, and gave orders that as rapidly as possible the bluejackets be sent by motor trucks back to the navy yard and the naval training camp.

Shirley Ann wanted to ask Ma Belle more questions about her assistant and what she meant about the facts, but she knew she wasn't supposed to be listening in on her and mama's talk. In fact, if her mama knew that Ma Belle had brought her out of the house after the riot, she wouldn't hear the end of it. If mama got really mad, she would be sent outside for a switch.

Ma Belle had said it would be their little secret, though. Shirley Ann wasn't going to resist a rare moment to share a secret with Ma Belle, queen of secrets.

"Child, you don't know what forever is." Ma Belle sighed, finally relenting to the little girl's complaints. "Alright, come on over here for a second. Let me show you what I'm looking at. But you can't never tell another soul about this." "I pinky-swear promise!" Shirley Ann wasted no time hopping up from her spot in the grass and running the short distance

over to Ma Belle and the telescope, a big black tube standing a few feet above her on top of three legs spread out into a triangle.

"Slow down girl. You got to be real delicate." Ma Belle told her, pulling down, then steadying the shaft of the telescope so that Shirley Ann could see through it.

Shirley Ann squeezed one eye shut and looked through the small hole, pointed at the sky towards the sun. It took her a second to figure out what she was supposed to be focusing on, and then she saw it. A thick, unnatural darkness quickly moved through the sky, but only inside the camera's lens, like a little mini picture show playing just inside of it. Shirley Ann had never seen anything like it. Everything around her felt like it was far, far away from her, as she got lost in the scene playing on the camera.

The middle of the hole seemed endless.

bluejackets be sent by motor trucks back to the navy yard and the naval training camp.

Bluejackets Raid Shooting Galleries

Soon after the beginning of the trouble in Beaufain street, bluejackets are accused of raiding two shooting galleries. They are reported to have used these small caliber repeating rifles indiscriminately until midnight, proceeded up town and, as they went up King street, wrecked a colored barber shop. An army officer and a naval officer who happened along, took an active hand here and compelled the bluejackets to leave.

A Broad street motorman refused to stop his car at Marion Square, and bluejackets, it is charged, jerked off the trolley. They entered the car, took a negro out, beat him and then shot him down. Another negro was taken from a car on King street near Market and shot down. Persons in a fashionable restaurant were unwilling spectators of this.

No Accurate Figures On Casualties.

While the several thousand bluejackets were in charge of the town, excitement ran high, and wild reports circulated swiftly. At 1 o'clock this morning it was still impossible to get accurate figures with respect to the casualties. Police and hospital au-

Continued on Page 9, Column 2.

St Louis	79?
Cleveland	45?
New York	1.30?
Boston	32?
Philadelphia	51?
Chicago	51?
Kansas City	156
Richmond	15?
ATLANTA	9?
San Francisco	14?
Dallas	46

Statement by

Late today, Secre sued this statement:

"While the official treasury department $3,849,635,000 subscri on Saturday, unoffici the several districts without any doubt t erty Loan is alread subscribed, with making a determi gather in every po tion before midnigh

"Thus, for the f country has met t treasury department required, and the Loan organization proved its metal."

The only gauge cials could use in a timate subscriptions lated was provided the fourth Libert

Continued on Pag

"It looks like the sun is being swallowed!" she yelled, one hand squeezing the leg of the telescope as she stood on her tippy toes to balance herself, the other squeezing her grandmother's hand.

"That's right, little one. That's exactly what the ancient Maya people thought. Their name for a solar eclipse meant, 'eating the sun.'"

Shirley Ann kept looking into the lens, her nose scrunching up. "What? That's funny. The sun is so big! What could be big enough to swallow it?"

The older woman smiled. "Well, the Chinese thought it was a dragon. But nothing's being swallowed up, really. What it is, is the moon passing 'tween the sun and the earth at just the right time. That black hole that you see through the telescope is the moon blocking the sun. You know, the sun has been doing that since before you was born. Since before *I* was born. It does it every so often."

"What you mean, Ma Belle?"

"I mean it's just one of nature's way of keeping time, the cycle of things. Some things are already set in place to happen, long before they happen—we just waiting to catch up is all."

Shirley Ann thought hard about that, wrinkling up her forehead. "I think I know what you mean," she said, going to sit back down in her spot.

"Good. Because what you just saw in that telescope is something that hasn't happened yet," Ma Belle replied.

Something that hasn't happened yet.

Just like that. Now Shirley Anne was really confused. "Okay, wait ... How was I able to see something that hasn't happened yet, inside the camera, but not outside up in this sky?"

"Well, it's a sort of magic trick I can make the camera perform. You see, in twelve days, the eclipse will happen and only people in a place called Príncipe near Africa and a place called Sobral in South America will be able to see it. But I can make my camera see the eclipse before it happens. I can make a record of it, just like it's happening, right here. Right now."

Shirley Ann had learned a little bit about Africa and South America in her geography classes, so she was now highly confused. As far as she could tell, both of those places was way too far away to be seen by her grandmom's telescope, let alone into the future. It sounded like a tale straight from a dime novel or the comics her big brothers sometimes read to her.

"But what *kind* of a trick is that?" she asked her grandmother.

"If I told you the secret, it wouldn't be a trick, now would it?" Ma Belle said. With a sly smile, she turned back to the camera.

Shirley Ann laid back in the grass and gazed up at the sun. She imagined a tiny point spiraling out from its center, radiating outward and growing larger until it covered the sun fully, transforming into a perfectly round, gaping black hole. She called back out to her grandmother as the spiral hypnotized her:

"Ma Belle, stop foolin'! How you do that?"

"Stop begging me for something I'm never gonna give you. And don't you go around thinking the future can be all the way predicted. Nor is shining a light on the future always a good thing. All magic has a touch of chaos..."

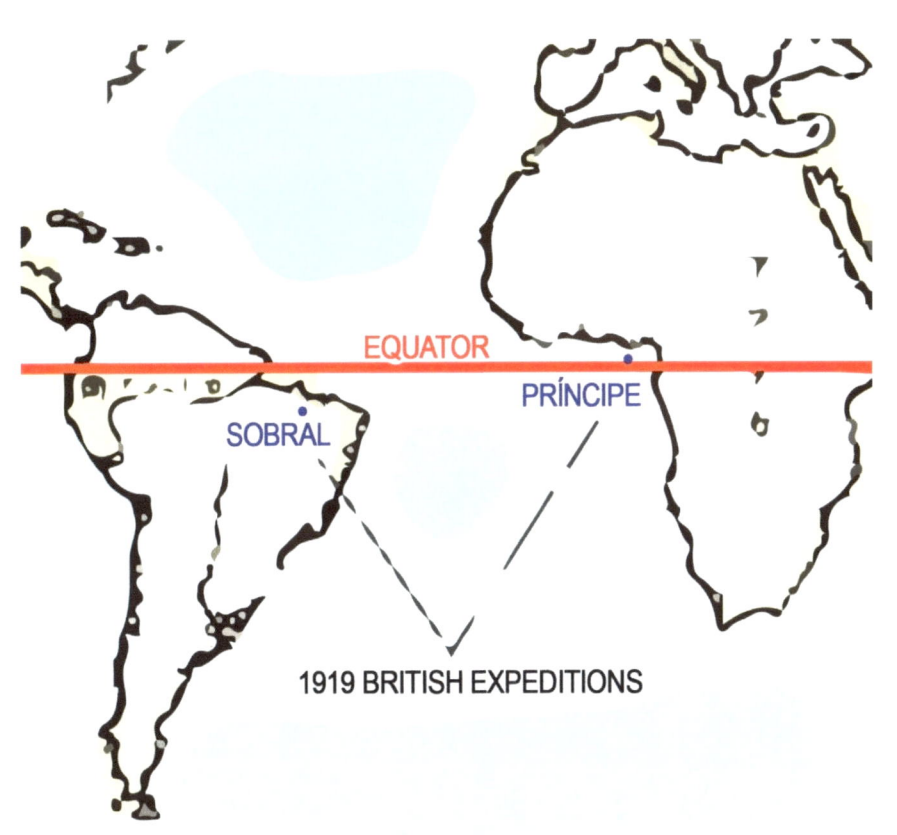

"At the quantum level, it is understood that what the observer will do in the future defines what happens in the past."

—John Wheeler (1977)

PHILADELPHIA, PA : MAY 15, 2019

"We know about your personal research, Smith." Kenneth Briggs, Managing Retrocurrence Coordinator at RCG, Inc., said as soon as the office door clicked shut behind him. Just minutes ago he had pulled Elaen A'roz Smith to the side, after the morning debrief in the Event Room, asking her back to the office for a "brief chat."

Shit. It was the chat she had been waiting nearly six months for. Of course they knew about her personal research, and anything else she did in her off time, simply by accessing the camera nearest her location.

But Elaen was still nervous, her heart thumping so loudly she thought they could both hear it as they took seats at her desk. RCG was made up of a small, but elite 15-member team of technicians, psychologists, anthropologists, researchers, forensic analysts. Among the three-person management team, Briggs was usually the "good cop" when it came to relaying difficult or unpleasant information to team members. But a good cop, bad cop, or any kind of cop felt threatening to her.

Briggs placed a red folder on the desk between them, what she knew to be a standard RCG dossier for an event manipulation. This folder was different in one regard. This one had her name—ELAEN A'ROZ SMITH—penned neatly in black along the top tab.

Elaen finally said aloud the lines that she'd carefully rehearsed for this exact moment. "Yes ... that's okay, right? I do it in my spare time, and it was research I was doing long before I came here."

Briggs nodded. "And we appreciate that you stuck to the policies about not using the company tech for personal use. Things could get too crazy around here if data gets cross-contaminated. You know all of the risks."

"Of course," she replied. The risks were infinite. RCG, Inc., also known as the Research Coordinates Group, had access to video and audio surveillance feeds from satellites, cameras and recording devices all over and above the known Earth. The devices could pick up on and remotely view virtually anyone's past or present actions, events, and/or conversations that were in earshot of a phone, camera, radio, monitor, or recording device. Everything from smartphones, laptop cameras, police dashboard and body cameras, parking lot security cameras, to satellite and GPS data feeds and google camera data.

They simply needed to pick a time, place, or person, and the event matching the data coordinates, and, using spatial mapping technology, could assemble the event into a 360-degree movie-like scene or Google map image, right onto their screens. All of this technology was then used by RCG to physically manipulate the information of public and private events that had occurred in the past: What some might call *fixing history*.

Using prototypes of the first quantum processors and first generation quantum computers discarded by Google and other companies, any search term that RCG input was instantly cross-referenced with any available internet, archival, university, government, and library databases worldwide, thus creating a more complete scene. RCG engineers would then automatically fill in or manipulate the details of a scene, video or photographic, with digital and holographic reconstructions.

RCG could go back to roughly the year 1875, based on images and footage from daguerreotype photos and the world's first homemade, moving images. The further back into the past the event, however, the fuzzier the data got, opening up the event to more possibility and randomness than could fit within the narrow margin of correction.

"Well, just consider this a check-in conversation," Briggs continued. "We are interested in your personal research and where you are going with it next." He gave a tight smile at the end of his speech, which did nothing to make Elaen feel confident that this was an innocent conversation.

There were several limitations to RCG's ability to "influence" events in the negative temporal direction. Technology and physics weren't yet advanced enough to break the perceived time, sound, and light barriers; manipulations remained digital and psychological, and physical in that they could erase all references and traces of an event from the internet and any digital media.

Because they couldn't *change* the event itself, only the photographic or digital remnants, and because they did not break any perceived physical time or sound barriers, they did not violate any known laws of physics. What RCG *could* do, however, and what they did extremely well, was manipulate history's perception of an event; which influenced the subsequent reality of the event. RCG usually focused on the smallest details of major events that would have an extremely calculated, within one percent accuracy, ripple effects. Big data and quantum computing helped RCG yield accurate predictions of the event manipulation on changes in the near and far future, including random quantum effects that they could seek to suppress. Manipulations and alterations were safe, subtle, and so seamless as to be invisible to the average person of average intelligence.

A really skillful Digital Fixer (known as a DFX) could manipulate an event with reverberations so minute and fine that even other DFX couldn't detect any difference upon reviewing the work. Of course the conspiracy buffs, internet message boards, and psychics noticed something every so often, giving it some cute name like *a glitch in the Matrix,* or *The Mandela Effect,* but there was built-in doubt to any of these claims.

The proliferation of fake news sites and "false flag" conspiracies after the 2016 presidential election only made their work easier. They weren't doing anything new really; photographs have been manipulated since the medium was invented, such as the 1860 picture of Abraham Lincoln on John Calhoun's body. Journalism was no more objective, principled, or reliable in the internet age than it was during the age of the printing press. RCG, Inc., just like the best historians, journalists, and scientists the world had ever known, simply worked backwards to make the data support the theory they were paid to advance.

"I know it's taken you some time to really be able to dig up the archives on your great-great- grandmother, Lula Belle Stout. There's not much out there." Briggs went on.

Elaen nodded. "That's right. Black women scientists in her time were virtually unknown because of racism and segregation," she said. "My great-great-grandmother was one of them. There's few records on her, but from what I've gathered, she was one of two black women who worked in the physics department at Penn for a few years. She also became an amateur astronomer and photographer after returning to her hometown of Charleston, South Carolina."

He nodded, as if he already knew everything about it. "And you've had your personal difficulties in your research, no?"

A shadow eclipsed her face. "Yes, I have," she answered, looking towards the file Briggs had placed on her desk, "but you guys already know all the details of my family history. I answered that in all the background checks."

THE "RED" SUMMER OF 1919

38 RIOTS NATIONWIDE

1919

Difficulty was an understatement. It was nearly a lifelong project that was sustained by the frustrating improbability of ever piecing together a full picture. Her own immediate family had little evidence themselves that Lula Belle Stout, the photographer or the scientist, ever existed. From what Elaen could pry from her grandmother Shirley Ann before her death in 2010, a house fire in Charleston, South Carolina had destroyed most of the family's belongings— including any photo albums, mementos, and records they kept.

Elaen decided to push back on Brigg's vagueness, wanting to get to the point.

"So, let me get this straight: You basically hired me under a pretense of wanting a skilled researcher, when all along you really needed information about my great-great-grandmom's work?"

* * *

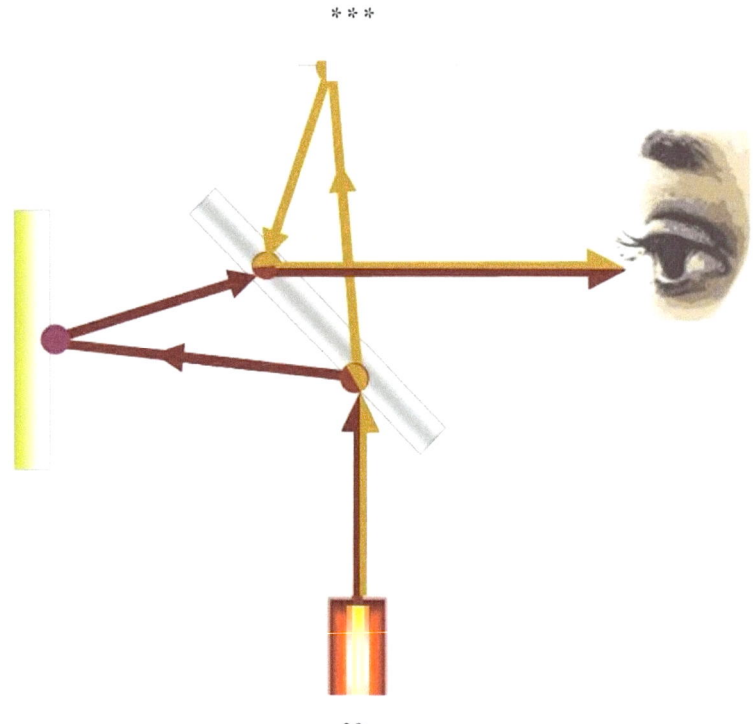

Elaen A'roz had been working at RCG as a retrocurrence coordinator for nearly six months. Her background was in cultural and social anthropology, receiving her Masters Degree at a small college near Charleston in 2016. She then returned to her hometown in Philadelphia to complete a PhD at Temple University, focusing on Philadelphia as the site of three race riots in July during the Red Summer of 1919, and teaching as an adjunct professor in the meantime.

It was at Temple one day, in late December 2018, where Elaen was approached by a woman, named Megan, who she thought was just another student in her seminar class of over 60 students. It turned out Megan was an RCG Inc. recruiter. Elaen was later surprised to learn that Megan had been in the class since the beginning of the semester, taking the mid-term and everything. Megan explained to Elaen that she'd been handpicked by RCG, as had all of her colleagues, due to her published work and exceptional anthropological skills. While she had several reservations about joining the company, including the way she was recruited, the sizable salary boost meant that she didn't have to make choices like paying rent over paying student loans for a few months.

A few months into her six-month probationary period as a part-time Retrocurrence Coordinator (RC) at RCG and Elaen had not disappointed. She was already considered to be doing an excellent job, according to monthly performance reviews.

Her background in cultural anthropology bought an unparalleled level of analysis to the events the group studied and manipulated—particularly those events involving Black and diasporic Africans in a range of socio-historical time periods. She was able to interpret cultural and ethnic-based objects, facial expressions, body language, and cross-reference it against an array of fields and archetypes to analyze what details in any particular scene a DFX should manipulate, what would be believable, and what wouldn't be.

But all of it was just a ruse to get more information on my Lula Belle, thought Elaen.

Briggs shifted uncomfortably and lightly cleared his throat before trying to regain control of the conversation. "More than that, Smith. We needed you, *need* you as a living link to her, to her work. And it needed to be the right time to tell you."

She had about a million questions—starting with just how long they had really been watching her, and maybe ending with whether they had manipulated data related to her family before. But, at the moment, all she could manage was, "The right time for what exactly?"

"Well, Lula Belle Stout didn't just have a passing interest in photography. And she did more than just calculate planetary orbits at Penn. We have come across evidence that gives our clients reason to believe that she was working on a theory of light and time that, had it been made public, would have supplanted Einstein's theory of relativity, or, at the very least, provided evidence that would have severely undermined it." Briggs stopped for a minute, allowing her a chance to digest what he knew would sound unbelievable.

And he was right, despite the nature of the work, her research, and the weirdness they saw on a daily basis.

Elaen A'roz laughed. "Wait, wait—is this some type of probationary prank? What do you mean?"

"I figured you'd think I was joking, but I'm afraid I'm dead serious." His grey eyes hardened into gunmetal and her smile disappeared. "There really isn't much time, you understand, so I'll need you to pay attention."

Desperate for more information, she nodded, her stomach knotting harder. "Please go on."

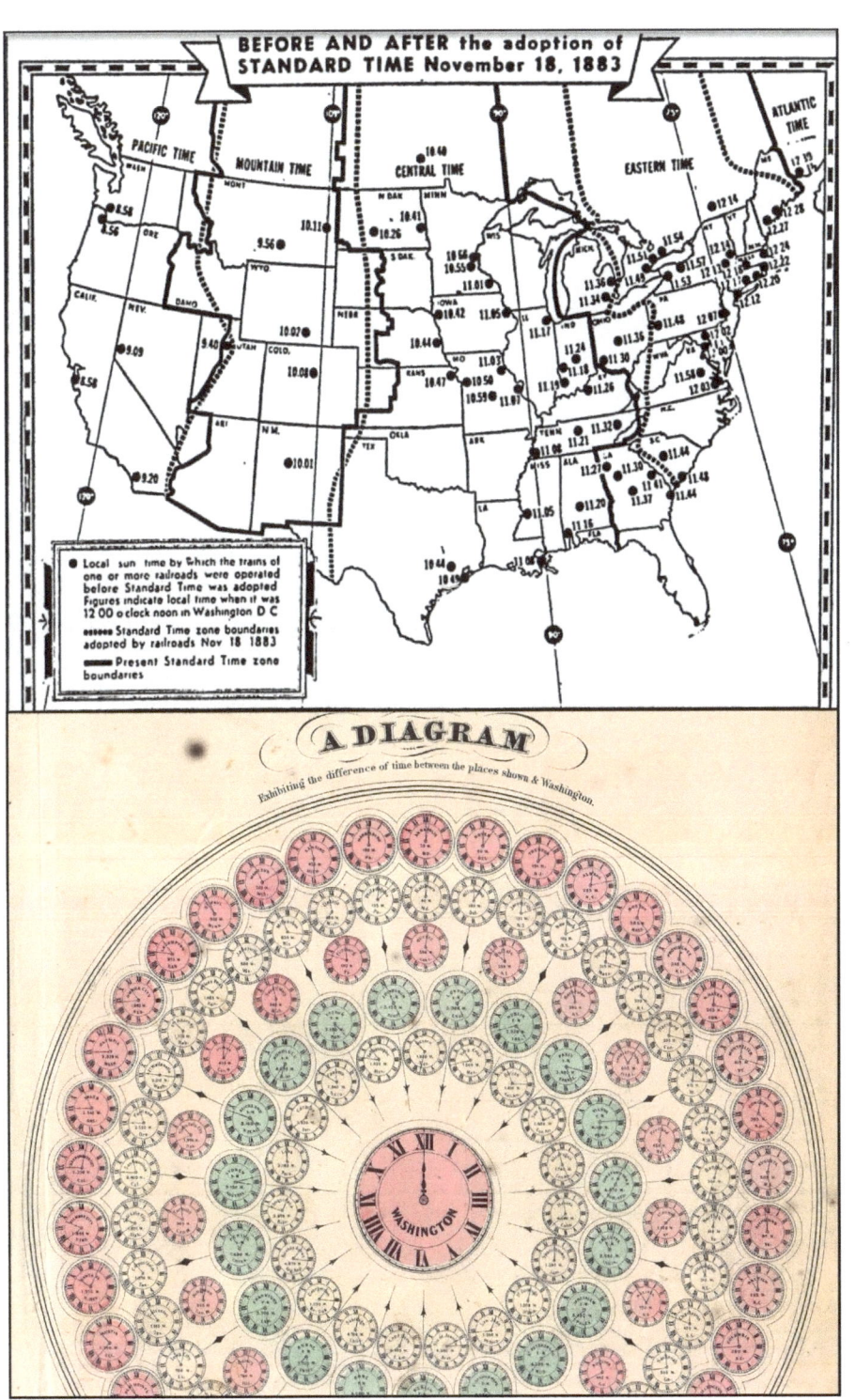

Briggs finally cracked opened the file between them, after pulling it closer to himself so that Elaen couldn't fully see its contents. He rifled quickly through the documents until he came across blown-up photographs of what appeared to be a solar eclipse, and handed one of the pictures to Elaen. There were points and measurements surrounding the eclipse.

Fig. 755.

Complete Panoramic Equipment.

"A few years back, a retired astronomer at the Neils Bohr Institute in Copenhagen found a box containing over 300 historic glass plates imprinted with images made from telescope observations, including lunar eclipses, comets, binary stars; some dating back to 1896. One of the plates found was from Edington's observation of the solar eclipse of 1919 from West Africa. I assume you are familiar with it?"

"Of course, it's one of the periods that my research is focused on," she said. "That was the eclipse that showed the bending of light. It was used to prove Einstein's general relativity theory and the curvature of space-time. In fact, the night of the eclipse was the same night as the race riot that took place in Georgia, May 29, 1919. But how would the eclipse, or Einstein, be connected to my great-great-grandmother?"

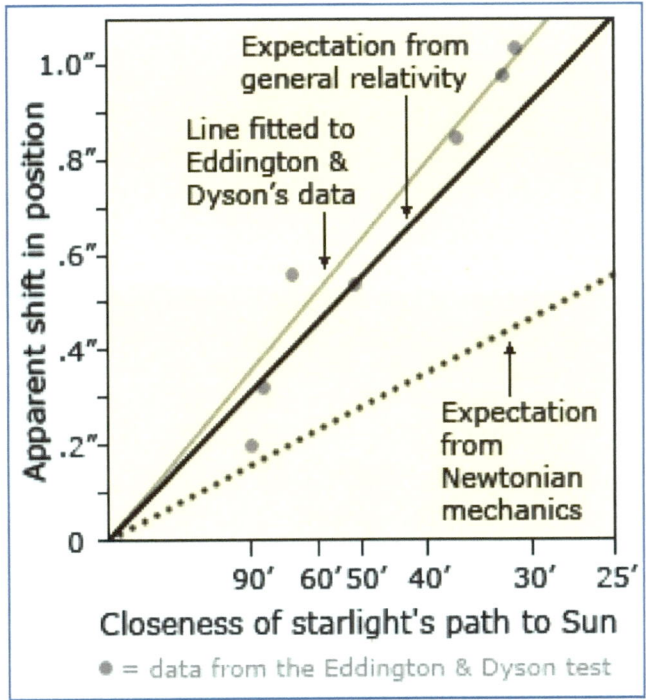

"Well, some of the astrographic plates found at the Institute weren't unwrapped and catalogued until recently, given their delicacy. There was one curious plate showing the eclipse—the same one that Eddington shot in West Africa. However, this plate was oddly time stamped for May 17, 1919. That's a full twelve days from the eclipse."

"And? That could have easily been faked or simply misdated, Briggs. We do this for a living."

"There's more, Smith. The plate was identified with the initials LBS. We have very good reason to believe that not only are those your grandmother's initials, but that she somehow captured the eclipse not only twelve days prior to the event actually happening, but in a place where she would not have been able to see it—from her home in Charleston."

Elaen gasped, then frowned, her rational mind grasping at her basic working knowledge of physics and the little bit she retained from training about RCG's quantum computers. "But that's impossible. What about violations of relativity? Even today's quantum physics hasn't been found to violate relativity yet."

Briggs gave her another pre-calculated dosage of information. "To be honest, we really don't know yet *how* she was able to do this. Stout was somehow aware of what we know today—that there are methods of communication that *appear* to function faster than the speed of light. Given her knowledge in physics, optics, and astronomy that was probably advanced for its time, she understood something peculiar about light speed and was able to somehow exploit light to bend back on itself in such a way that it loops information. She ... she was able to do this with a camera, somehow capturing images before they happened."

Total Solar Eclipse of 1919 May 29

Geocentric Conjunction = 13:06:29.3 UT   J.D. = 2422108.046173
Greatest Eclipse = 13:08:35.1 UT   J.D. = 2422108.047628

Eclipse Magnitude = 1.0719   Gamma = -0.2954

Saros Series = 136   Member = 32 of 71

Sun at Greatest Eclipse
(Geocentric Coordinates)

R.A. = 04h21m07.3s
Dec. = +21°30'16.0"
S.D. = 00°15'46.6"
H.P. = 00°00'08.7"

Moon at Greatest Eclipse
(Geocentric Coordinates)

R.A. = 04h21m12.6s
Dec. = +21°12'18.8"
S.D. = 00°16'38.3"
H.P. = 01°01'03.7"

External/Internal Contacts of Penumbra

P1 = 10:33:22.6 UT
P2 = 12:31:18.1 UT
P3 = 13:45:54.7 UT
P4 = 15:43:50.3 UT

External/Internal Contacts of Umbra

U1 = 11:28:27.5 UT
U2 = 11:31:29.6 UT
U3 = 14:45:43.1 UT
U4 = 14:48:43.2 UT

Ephemeris & Constants

Eph. = Newcomb/ILE
ΔT = 21.0 s
k1 = 0.2724880
k2 = 0.2722810
Δb = 0.0"   Δl = 0.0"

Local Circumstances at Greatest Eclipse

Lat. = 04°23.3'N   Sun Alt. = 72.8°
Long. = 016°42.5'W   Sun Azm. = 356.3°
Path Width = 244.4 km   Duration = 06m50.7s

Geocentric Libration
(Optical + Physical)

l = 1.70°
b = 0.40°
c = -11.08°

Brown Lun. No. = -44

F. Espenak, NASA's GSFC - 2004 Jul 12

sunearth.gsfc.nasa.gov/eclipse/eclipse.html

"Okay," Elaen said, taking a breath, "assuming this is all true, and I'm taking a huge leap of faith here, you understand, why are you bringing this to me? Why now?"

She could see him getting impatient with her questions, but she needed as much information as she could push him to give. She didn't know what they were up to yet, but if there was an event manipulation planned for this, it would mean her memory being assimilated into whatever the DFX manipulated.

And clearly he needed *something* from her, otherwise why would RCG have bothered revealing any of this to her? *They didn't even have to tell me they had this case* she thought. There had to be a way to leverage whatever it was they needed from her.

"Well we think we can take this thing to the next level," Briggs said "and really connect you to this event in unprecedented ways. You wouldn't just be analyzing a slice of the scene, like usual. Instead, you would become a part of the scene, navigating it like it's a virtual reality game, being able to really see the details of the—"

"But how could you think of having me be a part of *this event*," Elaen interrupted, "one that I happen to have virtually zero percent separation from? What about all of the risks you just came in here talking about?" *What could be so important about this job that RCG was willing to involve me and violate all of the company protocols that had been drilled into my head during orientation?*

RCG research and work was strictly regulated, so as not to cause undue interference. The team usually worked on large scale political events of massive or widespread significance. However, they could also change smaller events and the occasional freelance case—an actor or studio who wanted a disastrous movie to disappear, or a sports team owner who wanted a particular game wiped from the history booksonce heavily vetted by the executive team, who had to assure that the manipulated event had at least eight to ten degrees of separation from any of the employees of RCG, and nothing perceived as benefitting any employee or the company directly or indirectly. The executive team usually only revealed what details were necessary for the team to complete the job in their various roles.

It was only during an event debrief, typically taking place the morning after every event manipulation, that the team who worked on a particular event got to review their work in detail for accuracy, and still only learning such bare details as the place and time of the manipulation, but not the reason or outcome, and never the client.

It was because of this that Elaen A'roz nearly quit one month in, after working on an event with the team that tested the bounds of her own morality and sense of ethics. The event involved manipulation of digital records and photos from the 1973 murder of a young Black Panther, most likely murdered extra-judiciously by the police.

She had not known the exact details that the DFX would manipulate. She was present only to analyze a 5-second slice of the scene, and provide recommendation for the points of retrocurrence. After reviewing the slice of scene again during the debrief the next morning, it brought up a subconscious memory of an article someone had shared on her Facebook newsfeed about the non-indictment of a police officer who had murdered an unarmed teen about a year ago.

The question of whether the non-indictment had somehow been caused by the team's work, or just the inevitable, a part of the greater pattern of things, nagged at her all day. She spent the day writing her resignation letter in her head. What she thought she understood and knew so clearly: The cultural landscapes of historical events, the connections, configured into a self-constructed labyrinth that she stood at the center of.

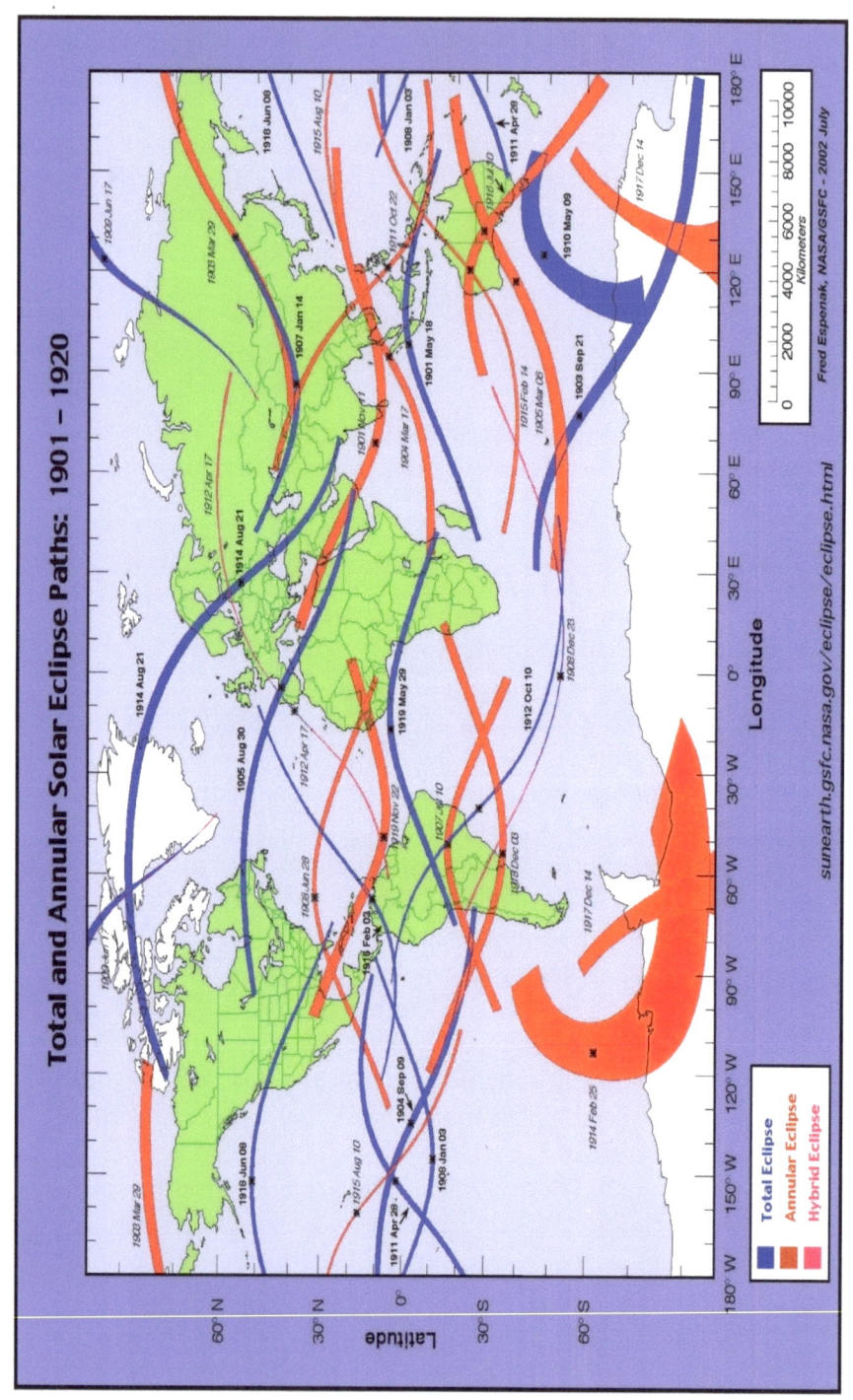

Total and Annular Solar Eclipse Paths: 1901 – 1920

Total Eclipse
Annular Eclipse
Hybrid Eclipse

sunearth.gsfc.nasa.gov/eclipse/eclipse.html

Fred Espenak, NASA/GSFC - 2002 July

Kilometers
0   2000   4000   6000   8000   10000

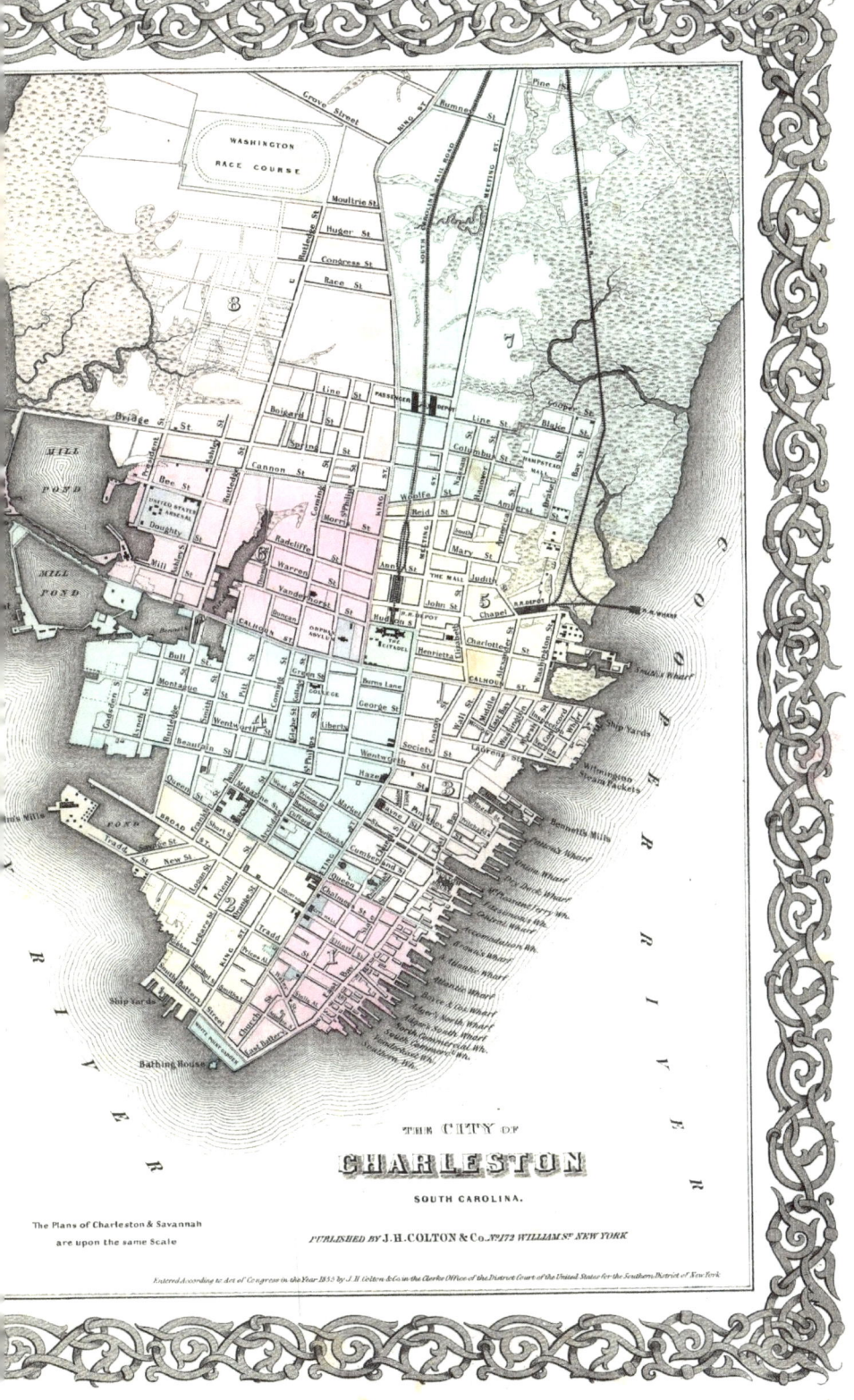

THE CITY OF

CHARLESTON

SOUTH CAROLINA.

The Plans of Charleston & Savannah
are upon the same Scale

PUBLISHED BY J. H. COLTON & Co. No 172 WILLIAM St NEW YORK

Entered According to Act of Congress in the Year 1855 by J. H. Colton & Co in the Clerks Office of the District Court of the United States for the Southern District of New York

By the time she got home that night, though, it had become hard to remember what had been done at RCG Inc. a few days before, or what effect it had on the world around her, good or bad. Part of her also understood that to be the inherent power of the company she worked for: to manipulate the collective memory, even her own, to make the rest of the world feel like whatever they manipulated was the inevitable, fixed-in-time outcome.

She had to accept a certain complicity in that power's potential ill-effects, effects she hadn't felt yet up until then. She also chose to forget her powerlessness, eventually talking herself into believing that nothing she would have done, or not done, could have saved the lives of those teens, either in 1973 or now. The resignation letter became a forgotten thought experiment.

Briggs nodded then, almost as if he could hear her thinking. "That's precisely it. Look Smith, you are here for a reason. You are like the mother of a new experiment here. Your connection to your great-great-grandmother puts us in a *really* special position. Your link to her, to her work, her experiences, is already is encoded in you, we are just facilitating the means. Science confirms this. Psychology and social science confirm this."

Elaen shook her head in disbelief, even though every word of it felt true. She looked down at the lines etched into the palms of her hands, curving and breaking like river courses on a map. Lula Belle's blood flowed just beneath, her legacy literally entwined with Elaen's flesh, linked across space-time through DNA.

And not just Lula Belle Sut alone. Elaen felt the link come alive every time she did her work. Her connections to the sites she studied felt almost visceral, like she had been there herself, breathing the air, hearing the sounds, smelling the smells. The memories of different places, distant timest, revisited her like they were her own experiences, when she allowed them to overtake her present senses.

Rasheedah Phillips

It was like communal memory through a needle, straight into her veins

And was what Briggs saying so far-fetched, at the end of the day, given what RCG did, what the company was? What she *did* for them? Things she had never dreamed possible, even with an open mind? She witnessed the manipulation of event memory every day of her time spent at RCG, had witnessed quantum technology change history as if it were rewriting a CD. There was no reason to believe this wasn't real.

"And RCG's end goal here is what exactly?" Elaen managed to ask, knowing there was so much that he was leaving out.

"Contain the situation, of course."

"What has RCG identified to be the *situation*?" She was starting to wonder if *she* was the situation. It was more than wanting her information on Lula Belle. It seemed as if they needed to have access to her very memories—psychological, biological and otherwise.

Briggs gave a quiet sigh. "Look, you know I can't get into any more of the classified details of this, and I've already given you way more than I would or should. At the end of the day, you need to treat it like any other job we get contracted for. You get minimal details. You remain neutral."

Containing the situation, at best, meant not having any of this revealed to the public. At worst, it meant manipulating the data, and eventually her memory of it, too. Most frightening of all, it meant manipulating her memory of her own family legacy.

"But you're not really going to ask me to remain neutral here, are you?" Elaen countered. "This is *my* legacy. Not only that, but you are asking me to blindly intervene with something that could have massive impl—"

"*Like. Any. Other. Job,*" he icily interrupted. Then, adjusting his tone, Briggs continued, "I'm going to level with you here. You're special. This is special. It's why I'm here talking to you. It's a huge job, it's sensitive, and you needed to be the one to do this. No one can connect to that scene the way you will, or handle it with the attention to detail that you have been ... bred, it seems, to have to this event."

She winced at his use of the word "bred."

In spite of her visible uneasiness, Briggs went on. "But let's be honest here. We can do this with or without your help or permission, you know that."

She detected the thinly veiled threat and knew he was right. If any of this were true, and their client were motivated enough, they could delete any trace of Lula Belle's work and completely discredit Elaen's work. She knew RCG *will do whatever is necessary to complete the job.*

But if she worked the event, she potentially gained so much more. Access to information about herself, her family.

And an impossible thought was beginning to brew at the back of her mind—that she could manipulate the event manipulation so as to neutralize RCG's effect. Or, at the very least, manipulate the event to be able to maintain her memory of it. She would figure out what to do with the information later.

"So I suppose I have no real choice?" After Briggs said nothing, she sighed as if defeated, thankful that, to her knowledge, RCG didn't have technology that could read her mind yet. "When do we do this then?"

Briggs curled his lips in a dry smile. If he knew she was up to something, he didn't show it. "In two days, of course. The 100 year anniversary of the date she took the photos."

* * *

Back in her small apartment near Temple University, Elaen had a day and a half away from RGC Inc. to prepare for the evet manipulation. At this point it made no sense to do much new or internet-based research, as RCG could easily tap into whatever she was doing on a computer, or whatever books she wanted to check out at a library.

She had signed dozens of waivers and authorizations prior to joining RCG that allowed them to do whatever was within the bounds of reason to ensure the protection of company secrets. Elaen also suspected they monitored her social media usage, and probably manipulated content algorithms like they did others connected to event manipulations. Everything felt suspect; the growing paranoia she had felt since working there, only amplified by the political and social climate.

One of the only advantages she would have in this event manipulation is her own unique perspective informed by her research, expertise in her field, and most importantly, her own life experiences and memories. It felt safest to stick to whatever resources she could find in her own home library and carefully catalogued system of notes, maps, and articles. She would have to shut down her laptop and feel her way through this by her own hands, material resources, and memories, the way her namesake would have.

She started off with cramming every article she could find on relativity, Einstein, Eddington, and eclipses. Elaen learned that the May 29, 1919 eclipse was a total solar eclipse, and one of the longest eclipses of the 20th century, clocking in at six minutes and fifty-one seconds. As Briggs mentioned, it was visible throughout most of South America and Africa as a partial eclipse. The eclipse's totality occurred through a narrow path across central Brazil after sunrise, across the Atlantic Ocean, with its end coinciding with the east African sunset.

It was on the island of Príncipe, an archipelago just off the western tip of Africa, where Arthur Eddington set up his own telescope and camera on a cocoa plantation, recording the eclipse at the point of totality, when the stars became visible. He also sent an expedition to the town of Sobral in Brazil, in anticipation of the possibility of uncooperative weather in Príncipe. The May 29th eclipse was to be a rare event—the Sun would be in front of the densest population of bright stars, the Hyades star cluster, providing a good source for measuring the light deflection.

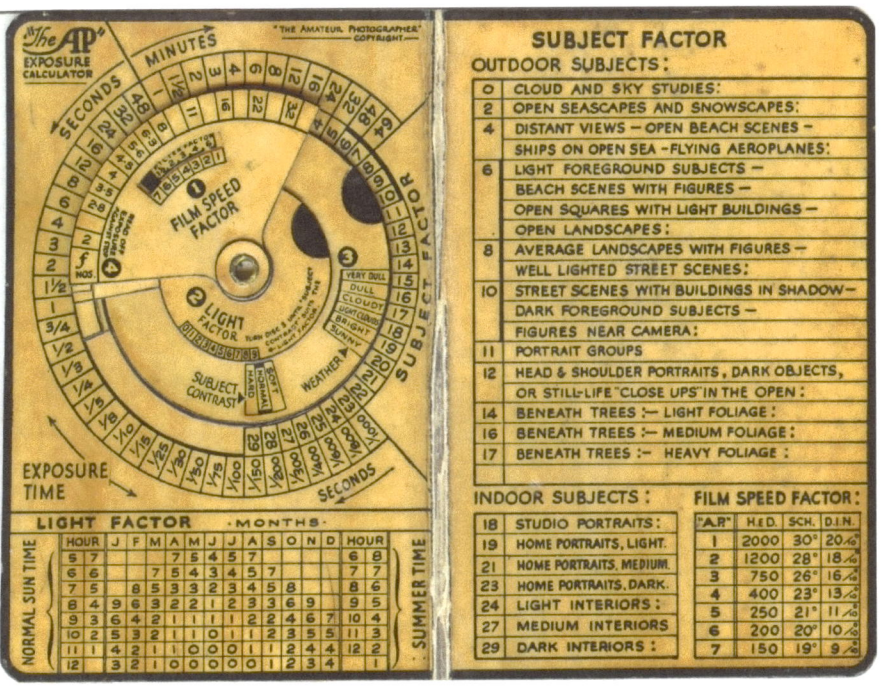

Several months after the eclipse, Eddington's observations came to be widely regarded as confirmation of Einstein's theory, given that he was apparently able to measure the bending of light based and compare apparent distances between stars, confirming one of Einstein's predictions about gravitational lensinges.

As Elaen dug deeper into books and articles, she began to remember the controversy surrounding the whole event. Eddington's observations were considered at the time to be near the limits of experimental accuracy. Some sources said that 85% of Eddington's data not agreeing with Einstein's theory was thrown out, while other sources noted Eddington's premature assessment of the photographic plates of the eclipse. The Sobral data was also insufficient; due to the intense Brazilian heat, the metal of the team's telescopes had become warped. Even some of the prominent astronomers of the time accused Eddington of manipulating the data. Elaen couldn't help wondering whether he and Einstein had the help of an RCG-like organization back then, as they would now, or if some retroactive event manipulation had caused the society in Einstein's relative future to regard the event with present-day suspicion.

An article Elaen had clipped from the Guardian newspaper back in 2012, titled "Why Einstein never received a Nobel prize for relativity" described how the Nobel Prize committee omitted the theory of relativity from Einstein's 1921 Nobel Prize for physics, due in part to the questionable data, as well as political reasons. While presenting the Nobel Prize the committee noted that it was being awarded without consideration of the value that his theories of relativity and gravity would have "after these are confirmed in the future."

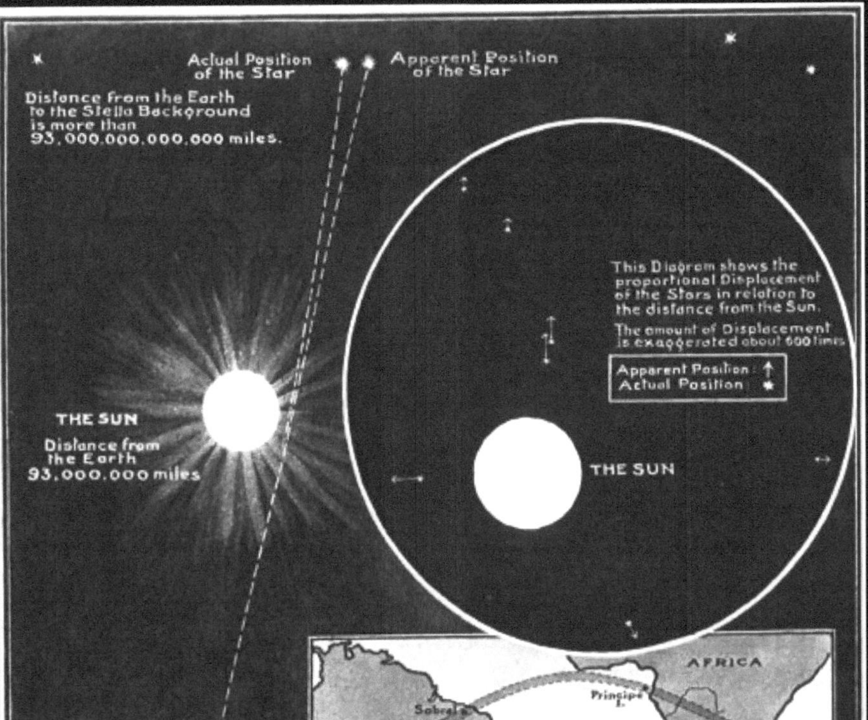

Actual Position of the Star

Apparent Position of the Star

Distance from the Earth to the Stella Background is more than 93,000,000,000,000 miles.

THE SUN
Distance from the Earth 93,000,000 miles

This Diagram shows the proportional Displacement of the Stars in relation to the distance from the Sun.

The amount of Displacement is exaggerated about 600 times.

Apparent Position : ↑
Actual Position : ✳

THE SUN

AFRICA

Príncipe I.

Sobral

SOUTH AMERICA

ATLANTIC OCEAN

Showing Path of Total Eclipse of May 28-29, 1919, and positions of the two Observation Stations.

THE OBSERVATION STATION AT SOBRAL, IN BRAZIL

The Corona

One of the more interesting facts that she came across was that the weather in Príncipe was cloudy, rainy, and 97 degrees Fahrenheit on May 29, 1919. Though it eventually cleared up by the time of the eclipse, there was reportedly a partial cloud at Príncipe which allowed Eddington to take only two clear astrographic plates.

Elaen knew such weather to be characteristic of Príncipe in previously researching the island (and neighboring island, São Tomé). Elaen had studied Príncipe's early role in the TransAtlantic slave trade as a primary transit point for ships, a major source for sugar production, and a prototype for plantation complexes in the South, as well as the lineage of maroons on the island. Because of the island's harsh terrain, maroon warriors who attacked settlers and plantations, tropical diseases, and the difficulties of growing food there, the island gained a reputation as "the white man's grave."

Príncipe and São Tomé were also once known as the islands in the middle of the world, being that the equator ran right through Príncipe on the south coast, while the prime meridian was but just a few degrees to the west. From what Elaen understood, Príncipe was particularly important because Eddington needed to be near the point where the Earth's rotation would keep eclipse observers in the Moon's shadow for the longest observation window.

Elaen was beginning to see all of these facts and events in a new light, connections tunneling their way through her mind as soon as she began to lose herself in the culture and environment surrounding the events, all of the elements that pulled together to make events decohere in time and history the way that they did, made up of both earthly and ethereal, physical and metaphysical materials. The information was as if imprinted on a hologram in her mind, light falling on parts that were always there perhaps, but inaccessible, due to arbitrary or evolutionary cognitive barriers ...

VIOLENT MELEE AFTER SOLAR ECLIPSE; MAYOR BALKS AT TIME TRAVEL THEORY

RCG CFO BRIGGS DENIES ANY INVOLVEMENT

Residents of Southwest & North Phila. Insist 'Time Travelling Woman' Visited; U Penn Professors Call These Accounts 'Ludicrous' & 'Ignorant'

By JOHN M. McCULLOUGH

Philadelphia nodded an absent-minded greeting to Ole John Barleycorn when he came back from oblivion last night.

The evening may have meant the return of "good liquor" to some folks around and about these United States, but to Philadelphia it was just a new, threatening inhospitable Tuesday evening, better made for cardpl- petsliquor-than cocktails.

Only two or three of the large, centrality hotels had anything that could pass as a crowd. The tap rooms did not do much more than their usual business, and the clubs, almost without exception, were deserted. Many had to liquid-ate beverages of any description for sale, and others had small acquisitions upon which their membership made slight demand.

The restaurants had liquor, but those who partook of it appeared to be motivated by curiosity rather than thirst. Many, after exploratory sips, turned again to beer and pretzels.

Even an initiated observer would have to admit that Ole John's triumphal return was a flop.

Speakeasies did their usual Tuesday evening business, and down in the Tenderloin, bleary-eyed stumble bums forked over their nickels and dimes for a hooker or gin or rye without even contemplating a visit to the higher-priced legitimate purveying points.

High prices and the advance knowledge that the supply would be limited-these contributed perceivably to the result.

And then, of course—no one who really wanted a drink at any time during the past 14 years was compelled to deny his thirst if he really wanted refreshment—and had the price.

Such stirring about as there was appeared to be largely on the part of the "younger set" who were bedeviling their daddies for fireworks to celebrate the Fourth of July, 1919, when the enactment of the 18th Amendment sounded the first stroke of legitimate liquor's knell.

No bearded ancients rushed with tears streaming from their faces to grasp this necked glasses and tend prayerfully above the effluvent bouquet!

No self-devoured gentlemen

Continued on Page 6, Column 1

IT'S ALL LADYLIKE AND GENTLEMANLY IN TOWN'S 'SPEAKS'

But Blind Tigers Don't Do Much Better Than Legitimate Places

In speakeasy, as in restaurant, club and hotel, Philadelphia met of Repeal Night with lady-like and gentlemanly drinking.

Waiting and hoping patiently for liquor that they expect will materialize, the speakeasy proprietors conducted their business as during their usual three years past—quietly and unostentatiously.

So things returned into them to liquor last night's environment "all is well" and Pan-American observ-

Continued on Page 6, Column 1

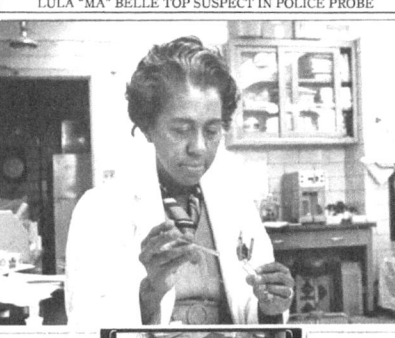

GOOGLE NEWS BLACKOUT ON ECLIPSE & RIOTS

Pass Through Bad Weather, But Report All's Well on Long Flight

NEW YORK, Dec. 5 (Wednesday)—A P—The Lindberghs, after hopping from Birchwood, West Africa, to Natal, Brazil, were 526 miles on their way—about one-third of the distance—at 3.5 o'clock this morning, according to a radio from their plane. The message mentioned "frequent squalls" and reported several skim, rain set and "wind over" at 1000 feet.

The message said at 9. Mrs. Lindbergh too...

Continued on Page 6, Column 1

OTHER KNOWN BLACK WOMEN SCIENTISTS EVADE APPREHENSION, POLICE DEPARTMENT PUZZLED

Addresses Legislature as Large Incomes, Holding G. O. P. Leaders Plan Companies Hit; Flat Normal Rate 4 P C.

CITYWIDE DRONE LAUNCH SCHEDULED FOR TMR.W.

Control Bill Again Voted; Final Action Is Up to Senate

TRENTON, N. J., Dec. 4 (Wednesday)—The State Liquor Control bill was re-enacted early today by the New Jersey Assembly by a vote of 31 to 11 overriding the veto of Governor A. Harry Moore.

The measure was sent to the Senate, where Republican majority leaders predicted its passage would make the law effect-ive immediately.

The bill was vetoed by Governor Moore last night...

PENNA. CONVENTION VOTES FOR REPEAL AS 34TH TO RATIFY

Copies of Resolution Rushed to Washington by Cycle and Plane

By JOHN M. CUMMINGS

HARRISBURG, Dec 5—Pennsylvania at 12.30 P. M. today became the 34th State to ratify repeal of the 18th Amendment.

Before a crowd that filled every inch of space in the imposing House chamber, the 71 delegates elected by popular vote in November assembly—and with due regard for the importance of the occasion—cast the ballots that put the finish as record for the 21st Amendment, with its provision removing the ban upon liquor from the Federal Constitution.

Continued on Page 6, Column 1

PRES. TRUMP ASKS U.S. TO GUARD LAW

Corporate Scientists Doubt Trump's Capabilities to Defend Violations of Known Space-Time Principles; Demands Military Tech Specialists be Put in Charge Indefinitely

By THEODORE C. WALLEN

WASHINGTON, Dec. 5—National prohibition came to an end at 5.27 P. M. today, Eastern Standard Time with the ratification of the repeal amendment by a State convention in Utah.

The official word was flashed to Washington by telegraph in three minutes and the adoption of the substitute amendment was formally proclaimed at 5.49½ P. M. by William Phillips, acting Secretary of State.

President Roosevelt, at 6.55 P. M. issued a proclamation revealing four special taxes yielding an estimated $212,000,000 a year and directing a "personal" appeal to all citizens to exercise their restored "dominion" of freedom in a spirit of temperance. The President called a meeting of his cabinet where he stressed "the state of emergence use of intoxicating liquors," the President urged the banishment of the bootlegger, the saloon, the illicit liquor traffic and the "repugnant conditions" of prohibition and pre-prohibition days.

Voices Faith in People

Declaring his confidence in the good sense of the American people not to bring upon themselves "the curse of excessive use of intoxicating liquors," the President warned that the return of the old conditions would bring living reproach to us all. Individuals and families were advised that they could contribute to the spirit of lawfulness by consuming only such alcoholic beverages as had passed Federal inspection, had paid reasonable taxes for the support of the Government and were dispensed through regularly licensed dealers.

The President asked especially that the States authorize no return of the saloon in any form.

He signed the proclamation in the privacy of his study and in the presence of only Stephen T. Early, one of his secretaries. The special taxes which it automatically repealed, as of dates varying between...

Continued on Page 6, Column 1

THE WEATHER

Official forecast: Eastern Pennsylvania—Rain and warmer tomorrow and colder in west; moderate to fresh south portion today; cooler tomorrow; fair and colder...

New Jersey and Delaware—Rain and slightly warmer today; tomorrow, fair and cooler.

Other Weather Reports on Page 2

MISSING PERSONS

LOST AND FOUND

Liquor Licenses Granted in Philadelphia and Vicinity

LICENSES for sale of liquor and wines in Philadelphia and vicinity were issued by the Pennsylvania Liquor Control Board today to:

Continued on Page 6, Column 1

In The Inquirer Today

Amusements	18
Birthday Bulletins	14
Bridge	19
Comics	21
Death Notices	18
Editorial	10
Hollywood—Louella Parsons	15
Local News	2 to 9
Obituaries	18
Picture Page	24
Radio	19
"Scala" Ham	17
Society	14
Sports	15 to 17
Stamps	19
Theater Movements	18
"The Love Waif's Son"	7
Travel	11
Weather	1, 2
Woman's Interests	14, 15

Proclamation by Roosevelt Decreeing End of Dry Law

WASHINGTON, Dec. 5 (A.P.)—The text of President Roosevelt's Repeal proclamation follows:

Whereas the Congress of the United States in Second Session of the 72d Congress, begun at Washington on the fifth day of December in the year one thousand nine hundred and thirty-two, adopted a resolution in the words and figures following: to-wit—

"Joint resolution proposing an amendment to the Constitution of the United States.

"Resolved by the Senate and House of Representatives of the United States of America in Congress assembled (two-thirds of each House concurring therein), that the following article is hereby proposed as an amendment to the Constitution of the United States, which shall be valid to all intents and purposes as part of the Constitution...

CONTINUED ON PAGE, 12 COLUMN 4

Apartments

The apartment you want to rent . . . at the price you want to pay . . . in the location you prefer . . . will be found in the "For Rent" columns on the classified pages of The Inquirer.

Turn to them now!

SCIENTISTS' VISIT LEAVES WHITE DEATHS UNEXPLAINED

"RETROCURRENT" EXPERT'S EFFORTS WORSEN CONDITIONS, CITIZENS WORRIED FOR SAFETY

JAILS MYSTERIOUSLY EMPTY

Sheriff's office confers with City Council

But Offer No Solutions or Plan of Reprisal

Lynch Mobs & US Marshalls at the Ready

Idling in Lieu of Appertainable Persons

It did seem at least clear that Lula Belle's photograph of the eclipse, as extremely improbable as it was, would have cast even more suspicion on Einstein's findings, had they come to light. He likely would have been further scandalized by the fact that Lula Belle was a woman, let alone Black. But still, the question of how, and better yet, *why* Lula Belle Stout had technology that could see into the future and across vast distances, and if she did, why she would choose to capture an eclipse still emerged foremost in Elaen's mind. Was she intentionally trying to disprove the theory of relativity?

Thoughts on Lula Belle's possible motives prompted Elaen to look back through her own records and notes on her family to see if any additional clues would reveal themselves. Ever since she was a child, she tried interviewing her mother Estelle and grandmother Shirley Ann about their family history, clutching a little tape recorder she got as a Christmas gift one year in one hand, and a pad and pen in the other. As she got older it became pushing and begging for more, but she learned very little outside of general dates of birth, locations, and scant details about how her grandmother Shirley Ann had ended up in Philadelphia.

Shirley Ann and her brothers and sisters were all born in Charleston and lived there up until the time a fire destroyed their family home. Because of this, Shirley Ann and her siblings were displaced and separated. Shirley Ann was raised in an orphanage and then foster homes, apart from her older brothers and sisters, and never made substantial effort to reconnect with them over the years. She moved to Philadelphia in the early '40s, lost her accent, and married a preacher named John Dewey. They had one child when she turned 35: Elaen's mother Estelle. Lula Belle, who was Shirley Ann's maternal grandmother, had been either estranged or had not been a prominent part of Shirley Ann's life—for reasons she wouldn't or couldn't share with Elaen during the times she'd pressed Shirley Ann for information on their family.

Shirley Ann was also legally blind and had been maybe all of her life—or at least all of Elaen's life. It was another thing that she wouldn't talk about. Elaen had never seen her walk with a cane, though, or ask for help. She always just said "I've lived a long time and I think I know my way around this world by now."

Estelle would go on to have one child of her own, Elaen A'roz Smith. Her mother had named after the great Zora Neale Hurston, but spelled backwards (pronounced E-lain-uh-rose). Elaen felt a gentle nudge all her life to follow in the footsteps of her namesake. Estelle had given birth to Elaen at age 40 after trying to have children for fifteen years with a husband who left her not too long after Elaen was born. He never looked back and they never looked for him.

Instead Elaen obsessed over her matrilineage, imagining herself spawned from a great line of mysterious Black women spread out through time back to Africa, with Lula Belle standing in front of the line. For many years Elaen resented her grandmother for denying her access to information that could put her directly in touch with that line, until she came to understand the painful and thorny roots of family legacies that kept many Black grandmothers silent. Shirley Ann had essentially come to Philadelphia to start a new life and break away from a past that had not been gentle to her. She passed away shortly after her 100th birthday, taking with her one of the few branches left on Elaen A'roz Smith's family tree.

Any other information Elaen had found on Lula Belle was acquired by going back to South Carolina, and spending months upon months during her free time, digging through records and archives at various libraries, historical societies, colleges and universities in Charleston. In fact, it was the very reason she had chosen Charleston as the place to get her Masters—so she could be closer to her roots.

Elaen didn't know what she would find, if anything at all, but guided by intuition and, what felt like burning desperation, she kept looking and looking until one day she found it, back in 2016—so small and faded she could have easily missed it if she wasn't using a magnifying glass. In a rare photo collection, in the dank basement of an unlisted, now defunct historical society Elaen had followed a trail to, she came across a single photograph of a building destroyed during the 1919 riot in Charleston, initialed by one L.B. Stout. Elaen cross-referenced this information with 1920 census data, noting 101 black women photographers out of 608 total photographers.

From there, she had been obsessed with uncovering what history had forgotten of her great-great-grandmother, piece by tiny piece. Combing through Charleston city directories from about 1895-1920, many of them missing, she found a Lula B. Stout listed in years 1902 and 1907, colored, with no occupation listed, living at an address that no longer showed up on new maps of the city. Elaen then had to go to old maps, to find the street where her great- great-grandmother's house may have been.

She picked up those maps now, reflecting back on that moment when she went to visit the place where Lula Belle Stout's house might have stood. There stood there now a shopping center, but even through the concrete floor of the parking lot, she could feel the energy of the past, from the ground up, waiting for stories to be unburied.

Further searches of census, birth and death certificates, cemetery headstones and will records turned up nothing of Lula Belle's existence, not unlike thousands of other Black women of her time.

Elaen wondered now whether RCG or its work had anything to do with this, either directly or indirectly? What else had Black women created or discovered throughout time that threatened the establishment?

(Reprinted from the NEW ORLEANS STATES)

3,000 WILL BURN NEGRO

Kaiser Under Stronger Guard Following Escape Of Crown Prince

Frank Simond
Writes For States

NEW ORLEANS STATES

VOL. 36 NO. 211   NEW ORLEANS, LA. THURSDAY, JUNE 26, 1919   LATEST NIGHT EXTRA

(Reprinted from the JACKSON DAILY NEWS)

JOHN HARTFIELD WILL BE LYNCHED BY ELLISVILLE MOB AT 5 O'CLOCK THIS AFTERNOON

Governor Bilbo Says He Is Powerless to Prevent It—Thousands of People Are Flocking Into Ellisville to Attend the Event—Sheriff and Authorities Are Powerless to Prevent It.

HATTIESBURG, June 26.—John Hartfield, the negro alleged to have assaulted an Ellisville young woman, has been taken to Ellisville and is guarded by officers in the office of Dr. Carter in that city. He is wounded in the shoulder but not seriously. The officers have agreed to turn him over to the people of the city at 4 o'clock this afternoon when it is expected he will be burned. The negro is said to have made a partial confession.

GOV. BILBO SAYS.
HE IS POWERLESS.

When Gov. Bilbo was shown the above dispatch, and asked what action if any he intended to take to prevent the affair he said:

"I am powerless to prevent it. We have guns for state militia, but no men. It is impossible to send troops to the scene for the obvious reason that we have no troops.

Several days ago, conversation

for the lynching has now been fixed for five p. m.

A committee of Ellisville citizens has been appointed to make the necessary arrangements for the event, and the mob is pledged to act in conformity with these arrangements.

Rev. L. G. Gates, pastor of the First Baptist Church of Laurel, left here at one o'clock for Ellisville to entreat the mob to use discretion.

THOUSANDS GOING

Elaen spent the next part of her research focusing on quantum physics, biology, and more specifically, DNA. Worried at first that she might have to get on the internet for updated research, she started rifling back through old articles and papers from undergraduate general education classes. She let out an audible sigh of relief when she found it—an article dated June 28, 2010 called "Quantum Entanglement Holds DNA Together, Say Physicists," printed out from the MIT Review for a biology assignment. Although the article's main thrust was that the the quantum effect of entanglement could be the thing that holds DNA together, what she found at the end of article that she had previously overlooked was even more interesting: "that the entanglement may have an influence on the way that information is read off a strand of DNA and that it may be possible to exploit this experimentally."

After a night of researching, she now knew what she needed to figure out before the event manipulation: if DNA is quantumly entangled beneath or within time, how could she use this link of layered instantaneous communication to actually communicate with Lula Bell in her own time? How could she warn her of what was to come, or rather, what was coming back to try to erase her work?

And she figured out how to do so in a way that would keep her linked to the event memory forever. She needed to leave an imprint so subtle, so quantum that RCG would not be able to detect it.

"The future enters into us, in order to transform itself in us, long before it happens."

—Rainer Maria Rilke

III. MAY 17, 1919/2019

In the Event Room, the team prepared to analyze the scene. A photograph of the eclipse apparently taken by her great-great-grandmother was queued up on the giant main monitor mounted to the wall at the front of the room. On either side of the main monitor were fixed five smaller monitors, displaying article clippings, documents, footage, and various pictures that would help set up a holographic recreation of the scene. Given the quick turnaround, Elaen had provided the RCG event team with a lot of pre-data to recreate the scene, a process she would not have otherwise had much involvement with, if any.

In the middle of the room sat a large, hexagon-shaped table with a holographic monitor embedded in its center. Briggs and two other members in the executive team sat in the Command room, a booth outside the Situation Room that gave them a bird's-eye view of the room, so that they could monitor all activities.

When Elaen was ready to begin, the table would render a 3D holographic scene as a three-dimensional snapshot of a moment in time ... using slowed down light, so that the scene appeared almost solid to the naked eye, and recreating the probable conditions of the scene where Lula Belle Stout would have taken the photograph, to as realistic a degree as possible, down to Lula Belle herself.

Although she could find no surviving photos of her great great grandmother, the RCG team was able to pull together what appeared to be a pretty realistic 3D holographic render based on backwards age progression of pictures of Elaen, her mother, grandmother, and any other distant relatives of Lula Belle Stout they could glean from the databases. Elaen was taken aback with how real the scene looked—it depicted Lula Belle Stout kneeling before what looked like a large homemade telescope.

In the middle of the room sat a device she had never seen before. Briggs had prepped her beforehand that she would be hooked up to a special machine called the psychotemporal transcranial stimulation device (PTSD, she thought without much amusement) that used a noninvasive method to stimulate several targeted brain regions responsible for memory and time perception. It was a form of virtual reality that was hyper-real, targeting regions of the brain responsible for short-term and long-term perceptions of time and memory, which allowed a user to functionally relive memories with sensations of smell, sound, touch, taste, and sight so real that it seemed you were actually experiencing the event in real-time.

The PTSD didn't look too much unlike a high-tech version of the hair dryer chairs she had spent countless hours under in beauty salons growing up. Where the dryer settings would be, there was instead a console with a number of unlabeled buttons spread out on its dashboard. On either side of the seat, was an armrest with cuffs attached, much like blood pressure cuffs used in doctors' offices.

As she sat down in the PTSD and put the helmet down over her head, a live, real-time feed of her, sitting in the PTSD, flashed up on the monitor on the screen before her, before morphing into the same scene of her great great grandmother that was showing on the monitor. Elaen relaxed in the chair with her arms in the cuffs, allowing them to tighten around her.

Elaen felt her consciousness squeezed into the size of a pinhole, as if she was being transported into the tiniest hole imaginable, in what felt like the blink of an eye. Everything went dark for one brief camera snap ...

* * *

I feel my mouth moving without my conscious direction, saying words that are not mine in a voice that I have never heard but which somehow still sounds familiar for reasons my brain has not yet caught up to.

"All magic has a touch of chaos." I say aloud.

... as the words leave my mouth eyes open, but something seems funny about what I'm seeing. I realize that I'm looking through the lens of a camera trained on an eclipsing sun and it dawns on me that I am ... I was ... am ... her... you ... me! Ooohhh my Godddd. I'm you....I'm..I'm here..

A voice in my head rings out as if its my own, except it isn't ... "You made it, I wasn't sure...There isn't much time left, young lady. The eclipse is only six minutes and thirty-one seconds long, and you're already late. I need the dates, locations of the next riots ..."

"Ma Belle! You ready yet."

I nearly knock over the tripod, I am so startled to hear a little girl's voice calling out a few feet behind me. I turn around to face her. And it was *her*. Not only was it her, but she could *see*.

"Ma'am, you alright? You look like you seen a ghost, Ma Belle," she says, sounding worried.

"Shirley Ann?" I am looking at the face of the little girl who will, in the future, become my *grandmother*. I see her through new eyes, who she has been, and superimpose that knowledge of who she will become. I see her eyes—beautiful, brown, round.

I wasn't expecting you to be here. We didn't render her into the scene. It slowly washes over me as I take in the vividness of the scene that I am here, actually here, not just analyzing the holographic scene. Otherwise how could my grandmother be here as a child?

...my granddaughter, child, don't look so startled now, you'll scare her...

I shake my head hard, feeling disoriented, in a state of temporal superposition. As I think, *I need you to give me the dates, locations, and death tolls for the next riots that will happen this year. We need to hurry, the window of time is closing with this eclipse, 90 more seconds ...* I feel my physical being-ness shifting, blinking in and out for what feels like a half second between the chair in the Situation Room, and here in 1919, in Lula Belle Stout's body.

Struggling to gain control over my senses, I feel a coldness rushing through every cell of my body, as if I had been submerged into a tub of ice and immediately lifted back out. *As if a ghost had walked through.* My mind is sorting through two streams of knowledge, *assimilating two presents into one*, trying to make sense of what she is asking of me 100 years in the past.

After what feels like the longest moment, it *happens.* I know what she knows and she knows what I know. I understand, I know now, that I have been prepared for this moment before I was even born. I know that the photograph of the eclipse twelve days into the future was not about Einstein or about advancing an alternative Theory of Relativity. RCG Inc, and its client had Lula Belle's motivations all wrong.

I began to read the locations, dates, death tolls, out to my grandmother/granddaughter in shorthand, "Okay, Shirley Ann, write this down, don't worry about the spellings. 5-slash-29, P-dot-C, G-dot-A. 5-slash-31, M-O-N-T, M-I. 6-slash-13, N-dot-L, C-T and M-E-M-P, T dot N. Oh no— oh no! How are we going to send two teams out on the same day, oh no, *no—!*"

"What, Ma Belle? What's all this mean?" Shirley Ann asked. I can hear her scribbling furiously on the notepad behind me.

"Nothing, baby, you just keep writing what I tell you." *I need the Philadelphia dates. Come on, come on. Get to the dates in Philadelphia. We have to warn our people there.*

I flip quickly through my mental filing cabinet for the Philadelphia dates and death tolls, knowing now why she needs it so urgently, each word spitting out of my mouth like bullets in an effort to catch the last information from the bent light of the eclipse. The information reads across my eyes like computer monitors, as I look into the center of the eclipse. I feel electric ... as the light writes the information over my eyes like a pixels across a monitor. With my grandmother's knowledge, consciousness, life experiences superimposed onto my own, I know how and why I am able to do this. Why am I here in 1919 and here in 2019 simultaneously. Why I know what I know, and why she always needed this to happen exactly as it. It's all in our eyes. It's perfectly constructed to read and interpret the language of the light; it contains everything we need already. The way the optic nerve bends the light, it looks just like how that star is bending light up there, doesn't it? In fact, what does that eclipse look like to you as it begins to fully cover?

I nod to myself, looking closer into the eclipse. It looks just like an eye. That's right. It's a good mimic.

And with that eye, I just stretch the reach of what I can see...
camera, the telescope, and a mirror. The mirror lets the light reach
to travel on the straight and narrow path.

The sun and the moon are both just portals for communicating::
how to exploit our ancestor's ancient, natural technologies.

You've created a disruptive gaze. It was surveillance turned back
giving rise to each other. I needed you here. I needed this to happen
exactly as it did.

I turned back to the camera to watch the last few seconds before
running out of time, but for some reason time felt slower
I would...this would happen? Did you pull me here?

... *The eclipse increases* the power; I just perfected its reach with the back in on itself, go around corners it other wise cant, since it likes

::We just learned

— in on itself, creating an infinite loop, turned in on itself, observing the observer, locked in gaze, the observed loop turned in on itself, creating an infinite loop, turned in on itself, creating an infinite loop

the moment of totality, I know Lula Belle thought we were in this moment, more exaggerated. But how did you know

UNIM
PRESS
LAYOUT
DESIGN &
FORMATTING
BY NEBRASKA
2017

A   A C

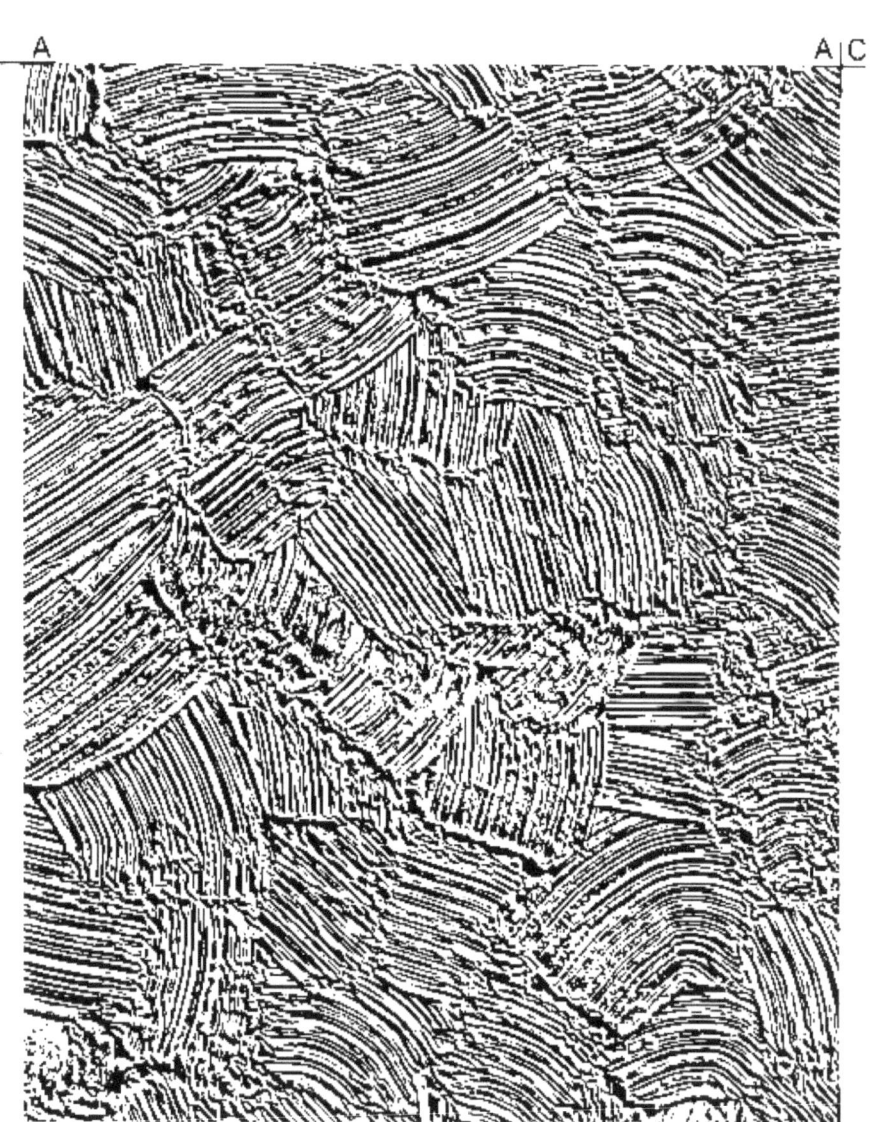